Santa's Claws

An Instalove Christmas Romance
Holidays with the Shifters Series
By
Rose Bak

SANTA'S CLAWS
© 2021 by Rose Bak

Table of Contents

About This Book

This year Santa is getting a Christmas present...a brand new mate!

Tony is transitioning back to civilian life after twenty years in the military and trying to figure out his next steps. When his mom signs him up to play Santa at Greysden's annual holiday festival, he's not happy about it. After so many years away from his family, he's lost his love of the holiday, and the last thing the grumpy wolf wants to do is spread Christmas cheer.

Marissa just moved to town, looking for a fresh start to heal her broken heart. When a growly Santa tracks her down and says he's her fated mate, she wonders if he's got some kind of brain injury. Humans don't turn into wolves, right?

Even crazier...falling in love with someone she just met. But is it real? Or just a Christmas romance?

About the "Shifters for the Holidays" series: The shifter town of Greysden is gearing up for the holidays and some of its sexiest residents are finally finding their true mates. The road to love isn't easy, but with a little help from fate and some nosy small-town matchmakers, there's a guaranteed happily ever after. If you love short and steamy standalone romances with curvy women and growly shifter men who fall fast and hard, this is the holiday series for you.

Get your copy of this instalove Christmas romance today!

Want a free book? Sign up for my newsletter[1] to be the first to know about new books and special sales. No spamming, I promise. Go to bit.ly/rosebaknewsletter to sign up for my newsletter and get your free book.

This book includes a special preview of "Until You Came Along", book one of the Oliver Boys Band series.

---

1.   https://storyoriginapp.com/giveaways/62ee758e-068f-11eb-904e-c373f6014fe1

Dedication

For everyone who believes in love at first sight – or love at first bite.

Tony

"I signed you up to play Santa next week."

I choked on my coffee at my mother's words. "What now?"

"You're playing Santa at the Greysden annual Holiday Festival. The usual Santa had to go out of town at the last minute, so I told them you would be happy to fill in so the children wouldn't be disappointed."

Yep, that still didn't make sense. I walked over to refill my coffee cup and give myself a moment to think before I responded.

"I'm not doing that, Ma. Forget it."

The sweet little woman who gave birth to me smacked me on the back of my head. Hard.

"Don't you talk back to me, Anthony Dean Capetti. It's already been decided. Your costume is in the hall closet. They'll be expecting you at the Greysden Community Center tomorrow at noon. It's noon to eight for five days, plus the lighting of the Christmas tree in the town square Friday night."

"I hate Christmas."

"Exactly. That's why you have to do it."

"Huh?"

"You need to get your Christmas spirit back, and this will help you do that. And it's a damn sight better than you moping around here like you've done for the last month."

"Moping?" I asked incredulously. "You've had me working on one project or another the entire time I've been here. I haven't had time to mope."

"You're staying here rent free," she reminded me.

I stifled a growl of annoyance.

"That's because you insisted, Ma. I was going to stay with one of my brothers, but you were all like, oh Anthony," I made my voice higher, imitating her. "You need your mother to help you transition back to civilian life, and I've missed you so much and I want you to stay with me so I can cook for you."

"That's all true, and it's also true that you've been mopey and at loose ends since you got discharged from the Army. Playing Santa will be good for you. It will help you remember how much fun Christmas was when you were a kid. I don't know what happened to make you hate Christmas but seeing the excitement of kids on the holiday will be good for you."

"What happened is I've spent the last twenty years in the middle of the desert fighting for our country, including every single Christmas since I enlisted. It's hard to be excited about Christmas after all the things I've seen."

I flashed on all the sad and joyless holidays that I had spent in the Middle East, eating reconstituted food rations, and opening holiday care packages from strangers. It had been as depressing as hell.

But now I was done with my service and ready to start my civilian life. I'd been lucky to get through so many years in the military without any major injuries, and now that I was eligible to retire with a military pension, I figured I should stop pushing my luck.

I just needed to figure out what my new civilian life would look like. I figured I would probably take the exam after the holidays to join either the sheriff department or fire department, depending on who was hiring. I had the skills for both, thanks to my time in the military, and I also had a veteran's preference for hiring. Active jobs like that would help me keep my wolf calm as well. He was used to constant exercise after all those years in the Army; an office job would drive him feral in a week.

We need a mate now that we're home, my wolf reminded me. *And pups.*

My wolf was right. It was time to settle down. I was almost forty and I needed to find a nice wolf to settle down with. Or any shifter really. I might not have found a fated mate, but I was sure I could find someone to build a nice life with here in Greysden. The truth was, I'd always wanted a home and family like my parents had.

"Well now you can fight for the spirit of Christmas instead of fighting for your country," my mother informed me in that way she had that I knew meant it was useless to argue with her. "Don't worry, I'll be there helping you."

I looked at her cautiously. "What do you mean?"

"I volunteered to be one of your elves."

"Jesus fucking Christ."

A tiny hand smacked me on the back of the head again. For such a little thing she packed quite a wallop. Damn shifter strength.

"Don't swear in my house, young man."

No amount of grumbling, negotiation, or pleading could sway my mother when she made up her mind about something, which is how I wound up walking into the Greysden Community Center the next day, dressed in a ratty old Santa suit that smelled like mothballs, and a scratchy synthetic white beard.

For her part, my mother was dressed in festive patterned tights, a long green tunic, a matching green hat, and shoes with jingle bells on them. She looked super cute, I had to admit, but only to myself. God knows I didn't want to encourage her. Like a lot of people in Greysden, she tended to go overboard about the holidays.

I looked around the community center, and I was flooded with memories of Christmas as a pup. My parents had always brought me and my brothers here for all five days of the festival and we'd looked forward to it all year.

"Hey there big guy, welcome back."

I accepted a hug from Gina Grey, one of the festival organizers. She had been about five years ahead of me in school when we were growing up, and she had babysat for me and my brothers a few times when she was in high school.

"Thanks Gina, you look great. How have you been?"

"Great thanks. I got mated this summer," she told me proudly. My eyes automatically went to the visible bite mark on her neck that told other shifters that she was taken.

"Oh yeah, I heard you and Drew are mates," I told her, referring to her childhood nemesis. "How did that happen?" Her battles with Drew were legendry when we were all growing up. It was pretty hilarious that the former enemies were now mates.

Gina waved a hand. "Ah, you know, you can't fight fate. Even if you try really hard." She laughed.

"OK I'll let your mom show you where to go. Your job is really simple, you sit there on your throne, talk to the kids to find out what they want for Christmas, let the photographer take a picture of you with the kid, and then your mom will move them along and send them back to their parents. Easy peasy."

Gina looked at me and sighed, "And for god's sake, try to look less threatening. I don't want to freak out the human kids. For some reason we've had a quite a few full humans moving in the last few years."

Greysden was primarily a shifter town, full of wolves, bears, tigers, and many other kinds of shifters, but we did have a few full humans living in town as well. Mostly the humans pretended that shifters didn't exist, and we overlooked the fact that they didn't have the benefit of living with an animal inside them like us shifters did.

Shifters are stronger and faster, my wolf helpfully reminded me. I rolled my eyes. He was a simple guy, my wolf. Very black and white in his thinking.

Ma got me settled into the Santa seat, which was basically a big wooden throne next to a decorated Christmas tree surrounded by brightly colored packages. I looked around while she conferred with the photographer. As usual, they had gone all out for the holiday. The organizers had turned the space into a replica of the North Pole. Well, the fictional North Pole anyway. It was a bit over the top; it looked like Christmas had thrown up in here.

The holiday festival was a beloved Greysden tradition. For five days the community center was transformed into a winter wonderland that included arts and crafts booths, food stands run by local restaurants, carnival games, and Santa visits for the kids. The festival extended outdoors into the town square as well, with booths and games lining the open area of downtown.

The whole festival was actually pretty cool, I grudgingly admitted. I had a lot of happy memories of the festival from when I was a kid. Maybe my mother was right, and it would be good for me to be out among regular people again. I scanned the crowd, looking for anyone I knew, and suddenly my wolf started going crazy inside me, clawing to get out.

She's here! She's here!

"What are you going on about?" I asked my wolf as I opened my mouth slightly and used my wolf senses to scent the area. The scent of cinnamon and oranges filled my awareness, making every cell in my body come to attention, drawing me in. Everything focused on that sweet scent. Could it be?

Our mate! We found our mate! We must go to her and mark her right now! Mate! Mate! Mate!

I struggled to control my wolf half as he tried to take over our body. I kept myself from wolfing out, just barely, but my animal was clearly taking control of my willpower in a way that hadn't happened since I'd first started shifting as a kid.

I stood up from my Santa throne, as if in a trance, and stalked across the community center, completely fixated as I followed the scent of our mate. I could hear Ma calling my name, but I was too far gone to respond. I followed my nose to one of the food stands. There she was. I sniffed again. She was human. It wasn't uncommon for a shifter to have a human mate, but it did make things a little more complicated.

My mate was a little thing, probably a good eight inches shorter than my six foot two, and all sassy curves. She was dressed casually in faded jeans that hugged her generous hips and thick thighs, and a form-fitting red "SG Catering" V-neck t-shirt that highlighted her cleavage. Her eyes were large and brown, her skin a pale ivory marred only by a scattering of freckles on the bridge of her cute little button nose. She had dark blonde that was pulled up into a high ponytail and, in a nod to the holiday, she was wearing a headband that had bouncing Christmas trees attached to little springs.

She was, in a word, adorable. She was, in another word, mine.

Ignoring everyone around me, I pushed past the line at the food cart and leaned over the counter to meet her startled eyes.

"Mate!" I growled.

Marissa

I felt the hairs on the back of my neck rise and looked up to see a seriously hot Santa shoving his way past the line to stand in front of me.

"Mate!" he growled, his tone possessive as he stared at me intently. I looked behind me, but no one else was there so he was definitely growling at me. Well, that was weird.

I had just moved to Greysden from Denver a couple of weeks ago and was working in the food court at the town's huge holiday fair. My old friend, Susan Grey, had a catering company in town and had purchased a booth at the event to serve the hungry masses.

I had just gone through a bad break-up and was ready for a fresh start. Over the years, Susan and I had worked together at two different restaurants so when I decided to get out of Denver, I gave her a call. I was grateful for the opportunity to pick up this part-time job while I figured out my next steps. Susan had already offered me a long-term gig working for her catering company if I wanted to stay on past the holidays, and she had also promised to put in a good word for me with the manager of the town's bar to help me pick up some waitressing shifts with them as well.

I wasn't sure if I wanted to keep waitressing long-term, but in the meantime, it was a good way to pay my bills. And most of the time I enjoyed the work. There was a lot of things up in the air, but I was digging the chance to make a fresh start. And it had all been going really well so far, at least until this guy burst to the front of my line and started growling at me.

"Mate!" he growled again. Honestly, it was the most animalistic noise I'd ever heard from a man. And what a man he was.

His Santa jacket was open, revealing a khaki green t-shirt that looked like it was painted on, clinging to the ridges of his abdomen and his muscled pecs. He had wide shoulders and a narrow waist and although I couldn't see much of his legs underneath his baggy Santa pants, I had to assume the bottom half was as muscled as the top.

He had olive skin, hinting at a Mediterranean heritage, and a bit of dark scruff shadowed his square jaw that was visible above the Santa beard that he'd shoved beneath his chin as he'd stalked over to me. His eyes were the darkest and most intense brown I'd ever seen, they almost seemed to glow.

I shivered and felt a rush of arousal. He was definitely the hottest Santa I'd ever seen. Too bad he was apparently crazy.

My friend and boss Susan came up alongside me, looking at the man curiously. "Oh, hey Tony, I heard you were back from overseas. How are you doing?"

"Mine!" he grunted, still staring at me with that intense look.

I looked at Susan in confusion. Her eyes widened as she looked back and forth between us.

"Oh," she said. "Oh!" She smiled like she'd just heard a great secret.

Before I could ask what was going on that everyone was suddenly incapable of using words that were more than one syllable, a petite elf came rushing up to join us.

"Anthony!" she chided. "What are you doing? The children are waiting for you."

"Mate!"

Did this guy only know one word?

"Mine!"

Make that two words.

The woman looked from Tony to me and back again, and like Susan her eyes widened and then she smiled delightedly. "Oh, wow."

Her nose flared as she leaned forward slightly, and I had the oddest feeling that she was sniffing me. "Anthony, honey, I don't think this is the best time to talk to the nice human about this."

What? Did she just say, "talk to the human"? With a slight emphasis on the word "human"? What was going on? Was everyone in this town completely nuts?

The guy – Tony apparently – didn't respond. He just continued to stare at me as I became increasingly uncomfortable. I had the oddest feeling of being prey.

I'd gotten lost in the woods once and some kind of wildcat had come up to me and given me the same look, like he was planning to eat me for lunch. I had shouted at him and sprayed bear spray in his face and that finally made him run away. I wondered if I had any bear spray in my purse. Maybe hair spray would work just as well? I was sure that I had hair spray in there.

The woman reached up and smacked Tony on the back of the head, which seemed to snap him out of his trance. He looked over at her and groaned, "Ma! Will you STOP doing that?"

She grabbed his arm and started tugging him away. "Susan will keep an eye on your...on this nice girl. For now, we all need to get to work. Come on now."

As I watched her drag him away, I felt the oddest sense of loss, which was so weird. I'd never been one to define myself by a man, and I didn't even know who this man was, or what on earth was wrong with him. So why did I feel sad as he walked away?

Maybe it was just because he was so incredibly hot. I mean, my god, I swear my ovaries twinged when he first looked at me. Yeah, that had to be it. This was all my hormones talking. It had been a few months since my last disastrous break-up, which would explain why I was lusting after the strange man who'd been staring at me and growling single syllable words.

"Is he, um, disabled in some way?" I asked Susan curiously. I was trying to be tactful in case he had a brain injury or something.

"No," Susan told me. "But it's a long story and we can't talk about it here. Can I buy you a drink after our shift is over and then I can explain?"

***

"Are you fucking with me right now?"

Susan smirked at me over the salted rim of her margarita. "Nope."

We had snagged at table in the back corner of Murphy's Bar, which Susan had assured me was the best place to get a cocktail in Greysden, and as I looked at my old friend, I was sure I had mis-heard her.

"You expect me to believe that the strange man is really some kind of a wolf man?" I clarified. "And he was acting like a weirdo because even though he doesn't know me from Adam, his wolf told him I'm somehow the perfect one for him?"

"His mate, yes," Susan explained. "I know it sounds unbelievable, but shifters believe that we each have one person in the world who is our mate, 'the one' as it were, and that is the person that the universe has determined is our perfect match. If you find your mate, it's like you find the other half of you, a part you didn't even know was missing until you meet that person."

"Did I hit my head and wake up in one of those Lifemark Channel holiday romance movies?" I asked as I took a huge gulp of my margarita. It really was delicious, the perfect mix of ice and high-quality alcohol. I would be a frequent customer here, I could tell that already.

I frowned as I replayed what Susan had just said. "We? You said, 'we believe'. Are you saying that you think you're a shifter too? Like do you turn into a tiger or something?" I scoffed.

"Of course not," Susan frowned. "Do I look like a tiger? Look at my build. Obviously, I'm a wolf."

"Obviously," I said drily. I wondered if I'd fallen and hit my head. Maybe this was all a concussion-fueled dream.

"You know I'm not light on my feet. I'm strong but not graceful. But my soon-to-be sister-in-law is a tiger and she's super light-footed."

"Of course she is."

"Have you really never heard of shifters?" Susan asked me. "I know we aren't super out there, but it's not like we hide who we are either."

"Well, yeah, I've heard the stories of course, but I thought it was like aliens or Big Foot, one of those things that only crack pots believe in."

Susan stayed silent for a few minutes, allowing me time to process what she'd told me. Suddenly a lot of things fell into place. Weird comments I'd heard over the years, the sense that there was some kind of, I don't know, magic or power or something in this town. The way that Susan was so freaky strong. I'd seen her lift cases of canned goods that even big guys struggled with.

Could it be true? Did shifters exist outside of romance novels? Or was this all some kind of elaborate joke?

"You're going to have to show me," I finally said. "I need to see this with my own eyes. Are you allowed to do that, or are there rules about this kind of thing?"

Susan put her drink down. "Let's go outside," she said, standing up. "We try not to shift in public, especially in a mixed crowd."

Susan hollered to the woman at the bar that we'd be right back, and I followed her to the alley behind the bar. She pulled her shirt over her head and handed it to me.

"What are you doing?" I squeaked.

"This alley is gross, I don't want to get my clothes dirty," she said calmly as she stepped out of her jeans. I turned around to give her privacy and she chuckled.

I heard some weird popping noises and then something bumped my legs. I looked down and saw a grey wolf. My eyes widened as I looked around the alley. There was no sign of Susan. Holy cow, was this really happening? Shifters were real?

"Susan?" I whispered, wondering if I was being pranked.

The wolf nodded its head like it understood me.

"If you're Susan, walk in a circle," I instructed, making a circle motion with my pointer finger.

I could have sworn the wolf rolled its eyes, but then it spun itself in a circle twice in one direction, then twice in the other direction, before coming to a stop in front of me and sitting on its haunches with an expression that clearly conveyed, "What are you going to do now?"

I leaned forward cautiously and stroked the wolf's head. Its fur was soft and thick and when the wolf didn't bite my hand off, I figured it must be true.

"Holy shit, you really are a wolf," I exclaimed. "Have you had your shots?"

Tony

"I need to find my mate!"

The minute Ma and I were done with our Santa shift I was ready to tear up the town looking for my curvy little mate. My wolf had been howling and scratching at me all day, begging me to make her mine before some other male claimed her. And now, she was gone. Her scent had long-since faded from the air in the community center and we were both desperate to track her down.

Mate! Mate! We must find our mate and mark her!

"Anthony," my mother put a hand on each shoulder and looked at me until I met her eyes. "You may have noticed that your mate is a full human?"

At my nod she continued. "Based on the look on her face when you growled at her, I'm pretty sure she doesn't know about shifters yet. You're not going to be able to just walk up to her and bite her and live happily ever after like you would be able to do if she was a shifter. You're going to move more slowly. You'll need to woo her a little bit."

"Woo her?" I asked in confusion.

"You know these humans, they like to date and get to know a person before they commit."

"But my wolf...he's tearing me up inside Ma, I don't know how long I'm going to be able to hold him back." Being away from my mate was causing my physical pain.

"You're going to have to," she told me in what I thought of as her firm "mom" voice. "How about we go grab dinner at the diner and come up with a plan for you to win your mate?"

"OK," I agreed reluctantly. It was a sign of how desperate I was that I was planning to listen to my mother give me advice about my love life. At least the diner had an excellent meat loaf so I could get a meal out of this little outing.

After a long sleepless night where my wolf was freaking out to find our mate, my mother and I headed over to the community center for our next shift, arriving just before noon. I really needed to find my own place, I told myself for the ten thousandth time since I'd been discharged from the Army. It was embarrassing being a thirty-eight-year-old man living with his mother, even if it was just temporary.

Although now I probably should wait and pick out a place with my mate. Her needs were of the utmost importance to me now that I'd found her. I just hoped she wanted to stay in Greysden. I would move if she wanted to, but now that I was back in my hometown around friends and family for the first time in twenty years I really wanted to stay here.

Greysden is a good place for us to raise our pups, my wolf told me approvingly. He sent me an image of my mate rounded with our pups, smiling underneath her Christmas tree headband.

"I think she only wears that at Christmas," I explained to the wolf. Holiday-themed hair accessories were not part of his world view.

I scented my mate the moment we entered the community center. My nostrils flared and every muscle tightened, ready to find her. My mother grabbed my arm before I could take off.

"Remember what we planned Anthony," she instructed. "Calm and non-wolfy. Be gentle. Don't freak the poor girl out."

I nodded and headed off towards Susan's catering booth, patiently waiting as Susan and my mate served the five people in line ahead of me. My claws extended, and I put my hands in my pocket as I tried to keep myself in control. Finally, after what felt like hours but really was only a few minutes, I reached the front of the line.

I hungrily took in my mate, once again overwhelmed by how beautiful she was. Today she was wearing another SG Catering shirt, this one in a dark green that matched the green and white Santa hat on her head.

"Hi," I said, getting lost in the brown depths of her eyes. "We, um, didn't get introduced yesterday. I'm Tony."

My mate paused for a moment, her gaze considering, then reached out to shake my hand. "Hi Tony, I'm Marissa. It's nice to meet you."

Our hands met and I felt a jolt of electricity run between us that was so strong we both gasped. Marissa looked down at our joined hands, her brow crinkled in confusion, and slowly drew her hand back and held it behind her.

"What'll you have?" she asked, her voice soft.

"Huh?"

Inside me the wolf rolled his eyes and chuffed in amusement at my lack of social skills around my mate. *Our mate wants to feed us. She is a good caretaker,* my wolf explained.

"Are you ordering food?" Marissa asked. She looked over my shoulder and I became aware that there was a line forming behind me. "This is a food cart. People usually come here to get something to eat."

"Oh. No. I, um, I wanted to ask if you were interested in going to the Christmas Tree lighting ceremony tonight?"

Marissa glanced at Susan, who nodded at her encouragingly, then looked back at me. "I didn't know about it, but yeah, sure, a tree lighting sounds fun."

"To be clear, I was asking if you would go with me. To the tree lighting, I mean."

I internally cursed my bumbling. I'd been less nervous when I asked Eliza Harrington to the freshman social twenty-five years ago. I wasn't the most suave guy, but usually I had a least a little bit of game.

She giggled, the sound sweet, and I breathed in her cinnamon orange scent. "Yeah, I figured that out. Yes Tony, I will go to the tree lighting with you tonight."

I felt a rush of relief. "Great, that's awesome. I just need to light it."

She cocked her head in confusion.

"As Santa, I do the first ceremonial lighting of the tree," I clarified. "We could meet here at eight o'clock if that's OK, then you can watch me do the lighting and we could, um, hang out after and check out the outdoor activities. I thought we could get some dinner and get to know each other. Does that work?"

She smiled and I caught my breath at how beautiful she was.

"Sure. I'll meet you at the front door at eight. See you then."

I felt like I was walking on air the rest of the day. I had a date with my mate, and anticipation made the day fly by. Even the brattiest kids couldn't annoy me today. I had to admit that my mother was right, asking my little human out on a date worked better than just growling at her.

Bite her. Mark her. Mate, mate, mate!

I reminded my wolf of my conversation with Ma yesterday. She might need some time to get used to us before that happened. We just needed to be patient while our mate learned our ways.

I hate being patient, my wolf grumbled. I knew how he felt.

As soon as the last kid went through the line, I rushed to the locker room to freshen up for my date. Unfortunately, I still needed to wear the stupid Santa suit for the tree lighting ceremony, but at least I could freshen up my deodorant and brush my teeth before we went.

Marissa was waiting out by the front door as promised. She had changed into black leggings, black knee boots, and a long white sweater with a loose neckline that showed off the delicate slope of her pale shoulder. She was carrying a black puffy coat for later when the temperature dropped. She looked incredible.

I rushed over and skidded to a stop in front of her.

"Hey, you came," I blurted out. "I mean, I'm glad to see you."

I mentally chastised myself for being such a bumbling fool. I'd led soldiers into battle. I was normally confident and decisive but something about my mate had me feeling unsure of myself. It wasn't that she made me nervous so much as I was worried about making a misstep with her and scaring her away.

"Should we head over?" I suggested.

As we walked to the square where the tree lighting would happen, I reached over and grabbed her hand, threading our fingers together. That same current of electricity ran between our palms. Inside, my wolf curled up in a ball, happy that we were close to our mate.

Marissa looked up at me with a smile and squeezed my hand. "I've never held hands with Santa before," she told me.

We made our way through the crowd to the small stage that had been set up near the town's holiday tree. The mayor waved as we approached.

"Tony, thanks so much for helping out," he said as he pumped my hand enthusiastically. "You know what to do, right?"

"Don't I just press the 'on' button?" I asked in confusion.

"Yes, and maybe give us some 'ho ho hos' and say a few words, if you don't mind."

I sighed internally. If my Army buddies could see me now, they'd be laughing their assess off. How did my mother get me into these things? On the other hand, if she hadn't bullied me into playing Santa, I probably wouldn't have met my mate so I should really be grateful I supposed.

The mayor started giving a speech and while we waited, two younger males walked past, giving my mate an admiring glance. I narrowed my eyes and growled at them in warning, sending them scurrying away.

You need to bite our mate now, the wolf ordered. *Tell the other males she is taken.*

I tugged Marissa closer and put my arm around her, then nuzzled her neck with my face.

"Are you marking me with your scent or something?" she asked in amusement.

I stiffened and looked at her in surprise. "What?"

She leaned close and whispered in my ear, "Susan explained. About the wolf thing. Also, I used to have a very jealous cat who did that to me sometimes."

Our eyes met and held. I saw warmth and acceptance in her brown depths. "Are freaked out about my being a wolf?"

"Well, not if you've had all your shots and you promise not to pee on my leg."

"What?" I reared back a bit and she burst out laughing.

"I'm teasing you Tony," she explained. "I admit it's all new to me, but suddenly a lot of things make sense. I realize I've been around shifters for years and had no clue. Susan was great, she explained everything and answered all my questions. I'm not freaked out, not about the shifter thing anyway. You turn into an animal sometimes, but it's no biggie. I've got weird habits of my own."

My heart filled with joy, and I resolved to send Susan a fruit basket or something to thank her. She really did me a solid by getting the shifter conversation out of the way.

I leaned forward to kiss my mate but was interrupted by the mayor introducing me. Well, introducing Santa.

"Stay here," I instructed. "I'll be right back."

I hopped up onto the stage, straightened my fake beard, and took the microphone from the mayor.

"People of Greysden," I boomed, figuring I might as well go big or go home. "I come from the North Pole to bring you tidings of joy. I declare that the Christmas season is now upon us. Let us join together to light the town Christmas tree and be merry! Ho, ho, ho!"

I looked down to see my mate laughing at my overly dramatic performance. I smiled back at her before hitting the "start" button for the lights. Standing this close to the tree, I was immediately blinded by the bright lights and stumbled back a step, nearly falling off the stage. Yeah, that wasn't embarrassing at all. Inside, my wolf was practically rolling his eyes at how ungraceful that was.

The crowd oohed and clapped as they took in the giant tree that was decorated with lights and decorations.

"Good job son," the mayor whispered, clapping me on the shoulder. "Thanks for helping out."

I nodded in acknowledgement and hurried back down to be with my mate.

"How'd I do?" I asked her. "That was my worldwide debut in the role of Santa you know."

She giggled sweetly. "You're a natural."

I reached my hand out. "Shall we?"

Marissa and I spent the next two hours wandering around the square. We picked up some hot dogs, curly fries, and hot chocolate from one of the vendors and moved to the heated tent where the town had set up picnic tables for the event. It was just below freezing, which was fine for shifters, but my mate was human, and I knew she would get cold if we ate outside.

We must take care of our mate, my wolf reminded me. *We must feed her and keep her warm.*

We found a table inside the tent and chatted easily while we ate our dinner. My mate was smart and funny and as we talked, we realized that we had a lot of things in common. We were completely focused on each other, ignoring everything around us as we talked and laughed and got to know each other.

We decided to head back outside and when we stepped out of the tent Marissa exclaimed, "Hey, look! It's snowing!"

She happily turned her face up to the flakes and I felt of rush of love that was so strong it damn near knocked me over.

I leaned down and kissed her softly on the lips.

"What was that for?" she asked.

"I know it's too fast and we don't know each other very well yet, but I'm falling for you, Marissa," I told her honestly. "My wolf has been going crazy since we met you."

She crinkled her brow. "Oh yeah, Susan told me about your wolf liking me."

"It's not just my wolf."

I leaned down and kissed her again, nipping lightly at her lower lip until she opened for me. My tongue swept in, tasting the hot chocolate on her breath as our tongues slid against each other. Marissa made a sound deep in her throat and moved closer. I wrapped my arms around her, holding her tightly, as the world fell away, and we kissed.

It was like one of those kisses you see in those sappy romantic movies. Everything stilled around us until it was just me and my mate, enjoying the world's most perfect kiss out in the snow. Or it was perfect until I felt something hit the back of my head, causing me to headbutt my mate.

Marissa

"Ow!" I pulled back from Anthony and rubbed my lip. "Why did you head butt me?"

He turned away with a growl. "Ma! What the hell? Why did you do that?"

A tiny woman dressed as an elf stood behind us with her hands on her hips, eyes narrowed and looking a bit deranged. I recognized her as the woman who'd pulled Anthony away from me yesterday.

"Anthony Dean Capetti! There are children here, and they don't need to see Santa Frenching his girlfriend! You'll traumatize them for life. This is a family event you know."

The woman's expression changed from irritation to friendly in a flash, and she leaned forward to give me a surprisingly firm hug.

"Hello dear, I'm Ida, this one's mother."

Oh, OK, this was weird, I wasn't used to total strangers hugging me, but I figured I'd just go with it. Greysden was a weird little town, that's for sure. It was nothing like Denver.

"Hello Ida," I said, hugging her back. "Nice to meet you. I'm Marissa."

"I'm sorry you were collateral damage, but I raised Anthony to behave better."

She him a stern glare and I had to laugh at the aggrieved look on Tony's face.

"So...have you two talked about anything important?" Ida asked, looking between us curiously.

"Susan already told her about shifters yesterday," Tony confirmed.

Ida looked relieved. "Oh, in that case, welcome to the family dear. You'll have to invite your family to join us for Christmas."

She hugged me again and I looked over her shoulder in confusion.

"Wait...what?"

"We haven't gotten to the mate conversation yet Ma."

"Susan told me about shifters and their lifelong mates too," I said, letting him off the hook. "Honestly, I'm not sure I believe it, but it sounds like a nice fairy tale."

Tony's face looked pained, and I did a double take, "Wait, are you saying that you think I'm your mate? We just met. Plus, as you know, I'm not one of you."

"I don't think you're my mate Marissa, I know you are."

"But...but how?"

"My wolf just knows. He knew the minute he smelled you, and we fell in love with you. That's how it works."

I cringed. His wolf smelled me? Was he saying I had B.O. or something?

"So, what? You tell me that your wolf whispers something in your ear and I'm just supposed to believe you? How do I even know that you're telling the truth?" I asked, starting to feel a little panicked. "Is this some kind of scam? Or something you do to fuck with the humans? Some kind of Greysden hazing?"

"What?" Tony yelped. "No, that's not it at all."

Ida rested her hand on Tony's arm to quiet him, then turned back to me.

"I know it's a lot to take in, dear, and that you're not yet familiar with our ways," she told me, her voice as kind as her eyes.

"I'm not completely sure how it feels for full humans, but I can tell you that when I met my mate I felt this immediate sense of calm, a sense of rightness, I guess. It was as if everything inside me stilled, and I could take a deep breath for the first time in my life."

Her eyes turned dreamy at the memory.

"I felt like I knew him, the real him, immediately. The minute he looked at me I felt like the most beautiful woman in the world, because to him I was, and every other man I'd ever met seemed to pale in comparison to him. I was more attracted to him than I'd been to anyone else in my life, and I couldn't think of anything else but him until we mated and completed our bond. It was...all consuming, yet it felt completely right."

My eyes widened as I realized that I was feeling that way about Tony. Could it be that what I was feeling was more than hormones or horniness? Were they telling the truth? I reached up to rub my temple. I was getting a headache. I suddenly felt panicked. This was all so crazy. I needed some time alone to think, to process everything I'd heard and seen in the last two days.

"I need to go." I looked around frantically, needing to escape.

"Marissa...," Tony reached for me, but I danced away.

"No, please Tony, leave me alone. This is all too much, I'm sorry but this just too crazy. I need some time to think."

I ignored the pang of guilt I felt seeing the hurt on Tony's face. "I'll talk to you later."

As I rushed away from the first man who'd ever told me he loved me, I felt like I was losing a piece of myself. I felt a physical pain deep in my stomach. It was like there was an invisible string pulling me back to Tony.

What on Earth was wrong with me? I wasn't some starry-eyed girl, and yet I was falling in love with some guy I'd just met who could change into a wolf just because he said I was his mate? My god, if I told anyone else about this, they would think I was completely insane.

After a sleepless night, I spent most of the next day on my couch, watching sappy Christmas movies on the Lifemark Channel since I didn't have to work. Really, it was amazing how many bakers named Holly lived in small towns and fell in love with corporate developers who wanted to build fancy condos in their town but changed their minds after learning the true meaning of Christmas. But as cheesy as the movies were, they kept my mind off my own problems.

I was no closer to figuring what to do about Tony that I had been last night. My heart and my mind were at war, and I wasn't sure which part would win.

The doorbell rang just after six that night and I frowned. Hopefully, it wasn't Tony; I wasn't quite ready to see him. It wasn't like he knew where I lived, but then again, in a small town like this it probably wasn't hard to find someone. I looked through the peephole and was relieved to see it was just my friend Susan. My friend the wolf, I amended.

"Hey there. Can I come in?" Susan asked when I opened the door.

I nodded, and let her in. She looked around, noting the holiday romance on the TV and the pile of junk food wrappers on the coffee table. So, I was a stress eater. It wasn't like it was that uncommon.

"Having a bad day?" she asked wryly, sweeping the wrappers into her arms, and tossing them into the trash.

"Tony thinks I'm his mate," I told her. "He said he's in love with me!"

She nodded. "Yeah, the fact that you two are mates was obvious to every shifter in the room when you first met. And that's why I told you about shifters, so you wouldn't be surprised."

"His mother wants me to invite my parents for Christmas after knowing him for less than a week."

I went into the kitchen and grabbed an open bottle of wine off the counter. I raised the bottle in question, and Susan nodded. I poured us each a glass and we sat across from each other at the breakfast bar.

"I get the shifter thing," I told her. "I mean, it's unbelievable, but I saw you change into a wolf with my own eyes, so I know it's true. But this soulmate thing. How do I know it's not just some scam? I'm just supposed to believe it's true because Tony says it is?"

"I won't lie Marissa, there are some unscrupulous shifters who tell women they're mates just to get them in bed or take advantage of them," Susan began.

"But it's actually pretty easy for other shifters to tell that people are really true mates. There's this, kind of invisible link between true mates, almost like you're tied together somehow, and other shifters can sense it when they're close by. When I was first met my mate Jonah, my sister-in-law and mother could tell almost immediately that we were true mates, even though I was denying it to them, and myself."

"But you're both shifters, right?" I asked.

Susan nodded. "Yeah, Jonah is a wolf too, but even when one of the mates is human it's super obvious that there's a unique connection there. Think back to when you met Tony. Remember how he just crossed the room and went right to you, like you were a beacon?"

I nodded.

"His wolf told him you were there, that you were his mate, and that's how they followed your scent." Susan confirmed. "And remember how his mother and I both looked at you and understood why Tony was acting weird?"

"Yeah."

"It's because we could tell what was going on right away. We could sense the connection between you. It's hard to describe really, but we just know, kind of like when something happens and you think to yourself, 'I knew that was going to happen' but you don't know why you knew? It's like that."

I twirled my hair around my finger as I thought about Susan's words.

"I understand being scared," my friend told me. "Before I met Jonah I'd been cheated on several times and I was afraid to trust that what I felt for him was real, even though my wolf was practically tearing me up inside to get to him. You can trust Tony, I promise you. I've known him since he was a kid. He's a good man. But what does your heart tell you, Marissa?"

I closed my eyes and thought for a second. The image of kissing Tony in the snow last night immediately filled my mind.

"My heart tells me that what you're saying is true, but my mind tells me that when I tell my family and friends that I met a guy and fell in love with him in two days they'll have me committed to an insane asylum."

"You already love him?" Susan sounded delighted.

I thought back on my words. "I guess I do. I know this is real life, not some romance movie, and yet..."

"And yet?"

I nodded as the truth filled me. "I feel it too. The connection. The bond. The love."

Susan jumped up and did a little shimmy dance that made me cringe. She might be a wolf, but she certainly wasn't graceful. It's a good thing she was a caterer and not a dancer.

"You've got to tell him, Marissa. That poor guy is so miserable he's making the kids at the festival cry instead of asking for presents."

"I'll go see him now," I decided. I looked down at my grubby pajamas and sighed as I brushed off some Dorito crumbs from my chest. "Well, maybe I'll change first."

Susan grabbed me and pulled me into a big hug. "I'm so happy for you Marissa. Tony is at the community center playing Santa until eight. Now get cleaned up and go get your fella."

Tony

A little boy kneed me in the nuts as he climbed off my lap, and I realized it was a perfect metaphor for how my life was going right now.

I was back at the Community Center for a shift playing Santa, but I was miserable. The bright lights and cheerful music all mocked me. After all these years traveling around the world, I'd finally returned home to Greysden and finally met my mate. I'd never expected to find someone so perfect for me and wasn't it just my luck that she didn't want me. I wondered if she would ever want me.

I knew it was a lot for a full human to take in, learning about shifters and fated mates. It was the stuff of human fairy tales. I just wished Marissa were a shifter. Everything would be easier then. She would understand what was happening between us, and she wouldn't fight it.

Our mate is perfect just like she is, my wolf said loyally.

It had been less than twenty-four hours since I'd seen my mate and already I felt like I was going crazy without her. Even though Ma had told me to be patient, to give Marissa some time to come to terms with everything, my wolf had been trying to claw its way out of my skin ever since she ran away last night. He didn't want to wait, he wanted to be with his mate.

As soon as we'd gotten here, I'd headed over to the SG Catering cart only to find out that my mate had the day off. I'd wound up telling Susan the whole story, pouring my heart out like some kind of a sap. A sap who would lose his mind if his mate didn't accept him.

I'd heard the stories of wolves whose fated mates rejected them. They eventually went feral and had to be put down. I wondered grimly if my brother Luc would put me down if I needed him to. That asshole had always had a chip on his shoulder about me. He'd totally do it. Ma would be upset, of course, but she would understand. It was our way.

After pacing around Ma's house last night until I was ready to scream, I'd finally called Luc and asked him to go for a run with me in the woods to try to calm my wolf down. I'd been afraid to go alone, worried that my wolf would take over and run to Marissa's house to mark her even if she didn't want us.

Luc had been more than happy to run me ragged, chasing me for hours, and then fighting with me after. I'd finally returned home at four in the morning exhausted and covered in bite marks. Luc was stronger than me, and twice as mean. He hadn't hesitated to beat my agitated wolf into submission.

The next kid jumped on my lap, hitting me in the gut with a surprisingly sharp little elbow. I sighed deeply, but then my wolf went still for a moment. I flared my nostrils, smelling oranges and cinnamon, and my wolf started racing around and freaking out inside me.

She's here! Our mate is here. Mate!

I struggled to keep him under control. The kid on my lap was a human girl, blonde and cute as a button, and the last thing I needed was to make another kid cry. I'd already done that a couple of times today. I couldn't take Ma smacking me in the head again. It was giving me a headache.

"Um, so what do you want Santa to bring you for Christmas little girl?" I asked, trying to smile beneath the scratchy beard.

The kid looked at me suspiciously. "If you're really Santa, why don't you know my name?"

"Um..."

"Santa is getting old now and there's a lot of kids in the world. It's hard for him to remember everyone's name without his list in front of him."

The little girl and I turned to see Marissa walking towards us with a big smile. She was wearing a short red dress with black boots and black tights, her blonde hair softly curled and held back by that ridiculous Christmas tree headband. She looked so beautiful that it took my breath away.

"Mate!" I breathed.

Mate! Mate! Mate! My wolf was as happy to see Marissa as I was.

"Hi there Santa," she replied, her expression hopeful. "Can I talk to you when you're done with your friend here?"

My heart started beating properly for the first time since she'd run off last night. I looked around her to see that my mother had closed off the line, leaving me free to talk to my mate when I was talking to this kid. Ma sent me an encouraging smile.

"I'd love that," I told Marissa.

The little girl gave me a list of about twenty-seven things that were "very important" for Santa to bring, then asked me a bunch of questions about my reindeer before she finally toddled off to join her waiting parents.

I crooked my finger at Marissa, and she approached my throne and to my surprise, she sat right down on my lap. I put my arms around her and everything inside me settled, including my wolf.

"Have you been a good girl, Marissa?" I drawled.

"I'm afraid I've been a bad girl Santa," she said softly. "I got scared and I ran away. I think I hurt someone's feelings. I only hope he'll forgive me."

"I think you get one free pass, but if you run away like that again Santa might have to punish you."

She raised her eyebrows. "Coal in my stocking?"

"Santa might just have to tie you to the bed and make you come over and over again until you never want to leave him again," I whispered, in case there were any shifter kids around. Those little buggers had good hearing.

Marissa wiggled on my lap, the scent of her arousal surrounding us, and I growled as my cock twitched. "Not the best place to do that, honey. This is a family event, you know."

She smiled. "How about we continue this conversation at my place then?" she asked.

"Your place?"

She nodded. "Rumor has it you still live with your mother."

I groaned. "I'm not living with her, living with her, I'm just staying with her until I get a job and figure out my next move."

"Well, how about we figure out your next move together?"

I stood up and slid Marissa to her feet. "Lead the way."

Marissa

I took Tony's hand and we walked hand-in-hand the few blocks to my apartment. My place was tiny, but it was home.

"This is me," I said as I opened the door and switched on the light. Despite my bravado earlier, I felt suddenly nervous.

Tony came around to face me and placed his hands on my shoulders, meeting my eyes with an expression I couldn't decipher.

"We don't have to do anything you're not ready for, Mate. I'm just happy to spend some time with you. We can watch TV or do laundry or just talk until you're to take the next step. I'm here for you, no matter how long it takes."

My nerves settled, as if Tony were imbuing his calm into me through his eyes, strange as that sounded. For some reason, his words increased my resolve. I popped up onto my tip toes and pressed my lips against him. The minute we touched, everything inside me settled. It was crazy to feel so much for him so soon, and yet, it felt right. I was done fighting it.

I licked the seam of his lips and slid my tongue inside, deepening the kiss. Tony growled deep in his throat, but seemed content to let me lead, and I threaded my fingers through the short strands of his hair, tugging slightly as I kissed him.

Our height difference made things a little difficult, so I backed him up to the couch and pushed him to a seated position. Hiking my dress up to give me some room to move, I straddled his lap. Tony growled deep in his throat as I pressed my already heated core against the bulge in his lap.

I slid his Santa jacket off, then pulled off the black t-shirt he was wearing underneath. My eyes widened as I took in his naked chest for the first time. Good lord, the man was ripped. He looked like one of the guys who graced the covers of the romance books I read when no one else was around. I traced his defined pecs with my fingertips, then followed with my lips.

"Take this off," he ordered, tugging at the hem of my short dress.

I shook my head, then leaned down and nipped at his shoulder. "Be patient, Santa."

He groaned loudly as I slid to my knees at his feet and began to unsnap his red velvet pants. Tugging them down past his ankles, I threw the Santa pants over my shoulder and admired the site of Tony sitting on my couch in his plaid boxers.

"I was right." I licked my lips and smiled.

He cocked his head. "Right about what?"

"Right that these Santa pants were hiding some fine-looking legs."

They were fine looking too, thick and muscular. "I've never seen you out of your Santa pants, you know. I was nervous that you might have chicken legs under there or something."

"Freaking Santa pants," he groaned, his voice aggrieved. "I...," his words cut off as I grabbed the waistband of his boxers and slid it down over his erection.

His cock popped out and bounced off his stomach, and Tony lifted his ass a bit so I could pull them totally off him. I threw them in the direction of the Santa pants. He sat before me, magnificently naked. I eyed his thick shaft and licked my lips.

"I love this," I told him with a smile. "You here at my place, naked and totally at my mercy."

Before he could respond I leaned down and kissed the very tip of his cock. It twitched, and Tony made a choking sound. I knew instinctively that he was holding himself back from his instinct to grab me and take over. I appreciated his restraint and rewarded him by closing my mouth over his engorged cock, sliding my mouth down as far as it would go and flattening my tongue against the underside.

I placed one hand on his knee and the other the base of his cock, and began sucking him off in earnest, taking as much of him as I could. Tony was making animalist noises and when I glanced up at him, I could see his fingers had grown into claws and were tightly gripping his own thighs.

Well, that was something you didn't see every day. I hadn't seen him in his wolf form yet, but I wasn't afraid of the transition, not after seeing Susan do it. I would have to ask him later to change for me so I could see him in his wolf glory. But not now, now I was focused on other things.

The idea that he was struggling to maintain control heightened my own excitement. I'd never felt so desired in my entire life. My nipples were painfully hard, and my panties were already soaked with my arousal.

I tightened my mouth around him, adding more suction, and moved to cup his balls with my other hand. His hips were punching upward now as he resisted his impulse to fuck my mouth.

"Marissa, baby," he gasped out. "You need to stop before I…"

I squeezed his balls, hallowed out my cheeks, and hummed simultaneously. He froze and then came with a shout, shooting warm jets of cum into my mouth. I swallowed rapidly, trying to get it all down, until he finally fell back on the couch with a sigh.

Pulling off him with a pop, I wiped my mouth with my hand then gave him a saucy smile.

"Well, that was fun," I said. And it was. Blowjobs weren't normally my favorite part of sex, but like everything with Tony, this felt different. Pleasuring him was all kinds of hot.

"My god, you really are perfect for me," he gasped. "Where's the bedroom?"

I pointed behind me and he leapt to his feet and pulled me up to standing. Bending at the waist, he threw me over his shoulder like I was a sack of flour.

"Hey!" I said, speaking to his naked waist.

"It's my turn now," he told me as he tapped my ass lightly and stalked to the bedroom. I wasn't a small girl, and I thrilled at how easily he was able to carry me.

Tony lowered me to my feet and dragged my dress over my head. I reached behind me to unhook my bra, letting it fall to my feet. His eyes widened as he stared at my full breasts in fascination, like he'd never seen a girl's bare boobs before.

"You're beautiful," he whispered. His hands snaked up to cup my breasts, his thumbs circling my nipples roughly. I moaned as waves of sensation traveled from my breasts straight to my already dripping core.

Tony pressed closer and kissed me deeply, his tongue dueling with mine. I felt him shove my tights and underwear down my hips to my thighs. Breaking the kiss, he lowered to his knees to remove them, but was stymied by my thigh-high boots.

I saw the tips of his claws extend and I tapped him on the top of the head. "Don't you dare cut my boots, Wolf Boy, they're my favorite."

He growled, and I giggled again. I had never been a giggler before, but I seemed to do that a lot around him.

I stepped away and sat on the bed, unzipping my boots, and kicked them off before lowering my tights and panties the rest of the way off and tossing them to the floor. I sat there naked in front of him, but I didn't feel at all self-conscious. How could I feel insecure when Tony was staring at my naked body like it was the perfect embodiment of every dream he'd ever had?

"What were you saying about it being your turn?" I purred, looking at him from beneath my lashes. "I'm getting a little lonely over here."

His eyes flared with heat. "On your back," he ordered.

I lowered myself to lay on the edge of the bed and he slipped underneath my legs, pulling them to rest on his shoulders. He stared at my moist pink folds for a long moment before surging forward. He licked me from end to end, slowly, and I squirmed under his mouth. His tongue was hot and rough as he tasted the wetness of my slit, humming happily. It was hot as hell.

Tony circled my clit with his tongue, moving around and around, then inserted one long finger into my channel. My back bowed and he gripped my hip to keep me in place, then added a second finger, stretching me.

He slid his fingers in and out of my channel and tapped the tip of his tongue against my sensitive clit again and again until I gasped, "Oh my god, I'm so close!"

He immediately sucked the bundle of nerves between his lips and bit down softly while bending the fingers that were buried deep in my channel. He hit a spot that felt incredible, and my orgasm hit me hard, harder than it had in my life. I screamed his name and then I was flying, totally mindless, the pleasure taking over my body as I shuddered my release.

Tony sat back on his heels and with effort I pushed myself up on my elbows, looking down at him. "Hey! You're kind of good at that!"

"Kind of?" he growled, pushing up to his knees and advancing towards me with a mock scowl. "I'll show you how good I can be."

I gasped and started scootching back on the bed, knowing he would follow.

"I would rather you show me how that monster cock of yours feels pounding in and out of me until I come so hard that I forget my own name."

His eyes widened at my dirty talk, and he hopped onto the bed, crawling over me as I made my way to the middle of the blue bedspread. I bent my knees and widened my legs to make room for him, and he slid his cock between my slippery folds, spreading my moisture on himself.

Balancing on his forearms, he looked at me with a serious gaze. "Are you sure Marissa? If I take you now, I'm making you mine forever. I won't be able to hold back."

"Once you mark me, it's like the wolf equivalent of being married, right?" I asked, recalling Susan's explanation of how mates worked for shifters. "You won't be able to look at another woman?"

"I haven't been able to look at another woman since the day I first laid eyes on you, Mate," he whispered. "I fell hopelessly in love with you the moment we met."

My eyes filled with tears. Never in my life would I have imagined this single-minded focus on me, the love and devotion I could see shining so clearly in Tony's eyes. Sure, it was fast, but who was I to say that "love at first sight" wasn't real? Or mate at first site, I guessed.

"Take me Tony," I said firmly, knowing in my heart I was making the right decision. I'd never been as sure about anything in my life as I was about this man. "Make me yours."

He moved forward so quickly he was a blur. I gasped as he thrust into me in one long push until he bottomed out inside me. We both stilled, breathing heavily as we waited for my body to adjust to his girth.

I felt my muscles start to relax and I tapped his shoulder. "Move now. Please."

Tony drew back, then slid in hard, and we both moaned. He repeated the motion twice more before he started pumping into me more rapidly, setting a hard pace.

"My god Marissa, you feel so good, you're so perfect for me, baby."

"Yes," I gasped as he picked up speed, moving so quickly that all I could do was wrap my legs around his hips and hold on. In and out, each thrust of his hips grinding against my pelvic bone until I was ready to come again.

"Tony!" I gasped as another orgasm hit me like a bolt of lightning. My god, I didn't even know I could come twice in a row like that!

Tony growled and I saw a flash of his extended fangs as he lowered his mouth to the juncture of my shoulder and neck. I felt a flash of pain as his teeth tore through my flesh, quickly followed by an overwhelming flood of love and contentment. There was an arc of energy and sensation and as impossible as it seemed, I could feel our souls connecting as he marked me as his. It was like every cell in my body was now in tune with his, his emotions as clear in my mind as my own. Even our heartrates seemed to sync up.

"I love you Tony," I gasped.

He released my neck, licking the wound a few times before he slowed his thrusts. He shuddered above me and succumbed to his own orgasm.

"Mate!" he shouted. "Mine!"

And as I felt him release his seed inside me, I knew it was true. I was his, and he was mine. Forever.

Epilogue – Tony

Six years later...

"Santa!"

I saw a little blonde boy toddle over to my Santa throne and I smiled down at him. "Well, hello there, little man."

I had been playing Santa at the Greysden Christmas festival every year since Marissa and I met. It had become a tradition, my mother and I working with the kids, and I had to admit I loved being Santa now. Not that I would admit that to my mother. My mate knew the truth though. I was a sucker for Christmas now. How could I not love the holiday that brought me my mate?

The Greysden Sheriff's Department was glad to give me leave for a week every year to work the event, saying it was good community engagement. It was definitely a nice break from giving speeding tickets and breaking up bar fights. The life of a small-town cop...

"That's not Santa, that's our dad!" Our five-year-old was not as impressed with my costume as his little brother was. He glared at me like I was trying to trick him. "I can smell you, Daddy."

Marissa squatted in front of our oldest, thinking she was whispering but of course every shifter in the vicinity could hear her clearly.

"Jackson, Daddy is helping Santa out this week because he was too busy at the North Pole to come today. He asked Daddy to fill in for him because they're good friends. Don't ruin this for your brother and the other kids, OK?"

Jackson looked between us then pursed his lips. "Fine," he grumbled.

Mason, our four-year-old, was totally oblivious to the conversation. That kid was our dreamer – always in his own world. He climbed up on my lap and crooked a finger at me. I leaned forward and met his serious brown eyes that looked so much like his mother.

"Santa," he whispered. "Can you bring me a little brother for Christmas? I'm tired of being the baby of the family."

My kids were the best. The last six years had passed in a blink of an eye, and I'd thanked God every day that I'd found my mate.

Despite her initial doubts about the speed of our courtship, Marissa and I had been incredibly happy together. We hadn't been apart for more than a day since we'd first mated, and we'd been married within a month. Our love grew stronger every single day and adding the boys to our family had just made it all that much sweeter. I loved our little pack.

I met Marissa's eyes over Mason's head and quirked an eyebrow. "Well there Mason, I'm not sure that's up to Santa. That's a decision that your Mommy needs to make. You should ask your mom what she thinks about your idea."

"Maybe Santa can bring you a little sister instead," Marissa suggested.

"No!" Mason said stubbornly. "I want a brother."

"Well, someone's going to be sorely disappointed," my mate muttered to herself, her hand going to her softly rounded abdomen. I looked up quickly, my eyes widening as I caught her meaning.

"Are you...? Does that mean...?" I stuttered in shock.

My eyes met hers and I saw the joy shining in their depths. We hadn't been trying, but honestly, I'd been hoping for more kids, even though I knew that Marissa wanted a break after having two boys in two years.

Shifter kids were a handful, and it had been exhausting for both of us having the boys so close together. I wasn't sure how eager she was to go back to two a.m. feedings and dirty diapers. But then again, I knew she'd hoped for a girl, and having a little girl who looked like my mate sounded like just what I wanted for Christmas.

Mason hopped down and wandered off to see what his brother was doing, and Marissa moved closer to me, giving me a happy smile.

"That's right Santa, we're going to have a little girl pup in about six months."

I leapt to my feet and drew her into my arms, kissing her deeply. A little girl. I couldn't believe it. I was the luckiest wolf in the world.

"Oh gross, Mommy's kissing Santa," Jackson shouted in the distance.

Suddenly I felt something hit me in the back of the head, and I flew forward, smacking my forehead against my mate's. Turning around, I glared at my mother in her ridiculous elf costume.

"Ow! Ma! How many times have I asked you not to do that?"

"You're in public Anthony Dean Capetti! Behave yourself!"

"Ma, cut me some slack. Marissa just told me that we're having the little girl that I always wanted."

My mother leapt forward and hugged both of us. "That's great news. I hope she looks just like Marissa and acts just like you. That will be the universe making up for everything you put me through Anthony."

"Hey! Don't jinx me, Ida," Marissa protested. "I never did anything to you."

"You won't be jinxed baby," I promised. "Our little girl will be just as perfect as you are. And I'll love her with every fiber of my being, the same way I love you."

She rolled your eyes. "You've sure come a long way from the guy who could only utter one syllable words," she reflected.

"That's what love does for you," I told her, giving her another kiss. "Merry Christmas, Mate."

"Merry Christmas."

***

Did you like this book? Show the love and leave me a review. Reviews are like puppies, they make you feel happy.

Coming soon: More great instalove romances in the "Holidays With the Shifters" series. In the meantime, keep reading for a special excerpt from "Until You Came Along", book one of the Oliver Boys Band series.

Special Preview

Until You Came Along by Rose Bak

Jen heard the rumbling from all the way in the kitchen. Wiping her hands on a towel, she walked to the front porch to watch the two large buses drive up the long driveway to the farmhouse. Belching smoke, they idled and came to a stop, one behind the other.

Although it wasn't even 10 a.m. yet, the sun shone brightly in the summer sky, showcasing the dust left in the wake of the parked buses. A bird squawked loudly in the sudden silence as a serious looking young woman scurried out of the first bus, glasses askew, a clipboard gripped in one hand, cellphone in another. Two large mountains of men followed her, hulking shadows.

"Jen Oliver? The band is here. We'll just come in and...." she moved to enter the house, but Jen stood her ground, blocking the door.

"Where are they?" she asked the woman, her tone icy. "And who are you exactly?"

The woman looked flustered for a brief moment before her stern mask fell back down again. She shuffled her cell phone into the hand with the clipboard and stuck out her now-free hand to shake. "I'm Simone. I manage the band."

Jen ignored her hand. "Well, manage them out of those buses. They don't get to send the help out to greet their sister."

Simone looked confused as she dropped her hand back to her side. "They're all sleeping. They had a late night. We'll just come in and check...."

"Still up all night and sleeping all day, huh? That's been the same since they were teenagers." Jen shook her head. On the farm they had all been taught the value of hard work – up before dawn, work all day, and early to bed. Somehow those lessons hadn't really stuck with her brothers despite her grandt' best efforts over the years.

Of course, the boys, as she still thought of them, had been away from the farm for ten years now, chasing fame and fortune as the biggest boy band to hit the charts since N Sync. Like the band that came before them, the Oliver Boys had grown up but continued to enchant teenage girls across the world with their pop tunes.

Simone clearly felt protective of the boys. "They played last night in Wichita you know," she said sternly. "The show went until almost midnight, then they met the fans and press for hours after."

"By meet the fans and press do you mean got drunk and partied?" Jen's tone did little to hide her opinion of the boys and their reputation for debauched partying.

Simone shook her head. "They've mostly settled down now. There's not as much partying as there used to be when they were younger. But they still need to make an effort to meet people, it's part of the job. Now we'll just come in and...."

Jen shook her head. "Well," she drawled. "When they wake up from their so-called job, you send them on in. The rest of you need to find some other place to bunk. I'm not running a hotel for drunken roadies here."

A slight movement behind Simone caught Jen's eyes. One of the giant men flanking Simone shook with repressed laughter, his mouth twisted in a smirk but his face otherwise impassive. Jen looked at him for the first time. He was the size of a small tank, several inches over six feet tall, with impossibly wide shoulders and large biceps. His hair was a dark blond, "dishwater blonde" her grandma would call it, worn military short. He was dressed all in black, and she noticed a gun on the shoulder holster. Jen wondered why he felt he needed a gun out here in the middle of nowhere. She felt him watching her and she raised her eyes to his, a shiver of awareness coursing through her, although she couldn't make out his eyes behind the dark sunglasses.

"Miss Oliver..." Simone started again.

"Jen"

"OK, then, Jen, we need to do a security sweep before the boys come in. If you could just move aside, we'll get started." Simone nodded decisively.

"A security—-what the hell are you talking about?"

Simone turned to the man who'd been staring at Jen earlier. "This is Nick, he's head of security for the band. He'll be doing a security sweep and assessment with Brian here," she pointed at the second silent man.

"We don't need a security sweep. This place is as safe as it comes. We don't even lock the doors in these parts."

Simone shook her head again, vibrating with irritation and clearly not used to people disobeying her orders. "No way. The boys don't go anywhere without a security check ahead of time. I'm afraid I have to insist."

Jen shot her a look filled with venom, her tone as cold as ice. "You can insist all you like but this is my property. You have no right to it, and neither do the boys. Y'all can just run along now, I'm not having some ginormous strangers poking around my property. Don't make me sic the dogs on you." Simone's mouth dropped open.

This was an empty threat. Jen's three dogs looked mean, but they were incurably friendly. They were just as likely to lick a person to death as bite them. Jen had a sneaking suspicion that if someone tried to kill her the dogs would jump over her body and leave with the killer. But these music people didn't need to know that. If there was one thing Jen hated, it was music people. They were way too self-important and proud.

"Excuse me ma'am," the guy called Nick interrupted.

"Jen," she repeated, a trace of irritation in her tone.

He inclined his head. "Sorry. Jen. As Simone mentioned, I'm head of security for the band. We've had some issues and I would be very appreciative if my team could just poke around for a bit and make sure there's nothing amiss." His tone was deferential and charming, which only heightened Jen's suspicions.

"What kind of issues?"

"I'm afraid I'm not at liberty to discuss that ma—I mean Jen."

"Then I'm afraid I'm not at liberty to grant you access to my property. You step foot off that driveway, and I'll shoot you myself, right after I set the dogs on you. And you," she pointed at Simone, "better make sure no one bothers me again until I see those boys on my porch." She spun on her heel and slammed the door. It was going to be a long day.

****

*For more of Jen's story, check out **Until You Came Along** by Rose Bak. Available at all major online retailers.*

Other Books by Rose Bak

Holidays With the Shifters Series
Santa's Claws
Bear Humbug
Bite-Sized Shifters Paranormal Romance Series
Wolf Doctor
Kat's Dog
Designer Wolf
Wolf Sheriff
Cocktail Wolf
The Diamond Bay Contemporary Romance Series
Brand New Penny
Fresh as a Daisy
Right as Rain
The Reunited Series
Together Again
Finding My Baby
The Oliver Boys Band Contemporary Romance Series
Until You Came Along
Rock Star Teacher
Rock Star Writer
Rock Star Neighbor
Loving the Holidays Contemporary Romance Series
Dating Santa
New Year's Steve
Independence Dave
The Good with Numbers Holiday Romance Series
Love Unmasked
The Thanksgiving Scrooge
Maid for Christmas
Countdown to Love

Valentine's Lottery
Beach Wedding
Non-fiction
What to Do If You Find a Cougar in Your Living Room: Self-Care in an Uncaring World
Catch up with these and other stories coming soon. Join my newsletter for more information[1] or follow my author page on your favorite retailer.

---

1.   https://storyoriginapp.com/giveaways/62ee758e-068f-11eb-904e-c373f6014fe1

About the Author

Rose Bak has been obsessed with books since she got her first library card at age five. She is a passionate reader with an e-reader bursting with thousands of beloved books.

Although Rose enjoys writing both fiction and nonfiction, romance novels have always been her favorite guilty pleasure, both as a reader and an author. Rose's contemporary romance books focus on strong female characters over age 35 and the alpha males who love them. Expect a lot of steam, a little bit of snark, and a guaranteed happily ever after.

Rose lives in the Pacific Northwest with her family, and special needs dogs. In addition to writing, she also teaches accessible yoga and loves music. Sadly, she has absolutely no musical talent, so she mostly sings in the shower.

Please sign up for Rose's newsletter[1] at bit.ly/rosebaknewsletter to get a free book and keep up to date on all the latest news.

---

1. *https://storyoriginapp.com/giveaways/62ee758e-068f-11eb-904e-c373f6014fe1*

Don't miss out!

Visit the website below and you can sign up to receive emails whenever Rose Bak publishes a new book. There's no charge and no obligation.

https://books2read.com/r/B-A-VATM-MRYSB

Connecting independent readers to independent writers.

Did you love *Santa's Claws*? Then you should read *Bear Humbug*[2] by Rose Bak!

Is there something in the water in the town of Greysden? Because falling in love within days of meeting someone isn't normal. And neither is seeing a bear turn into an incredibly attractive man...

When she learns that her best friend has fallen in love with a guy she just met, April is determined to save her from whatever weird cult has captured her. She doesn't find a cult, but she does find a growly, Christmas-hating bear shifter who insists that April is his fated mate.

A family tragedy years ago made Tyler hate Christmas and convinced him that he should avoid having a mate at all costs. He doesn't care that his bear is insisting the woman who just pepper sprayed him is the one

---

2. https://books2read.com/u/mYGXoo

3. https://books2read.com/u/mYGXoo

they're meant to be with forever. He's just going to avoid her until the holidays are over and leaves town.

Unfortunately, fate has other plans...

About the "Shifters for the Holidays" series: The shifter town of Greysden is gearing up for the holidays and some of its sexiest residents are finally finding their true mates. The road to love isn't easy, but with a little help from fate and some nosy small-town matchmakers, there's a guaranteed happily ever after. If you love short and steamy standalone romances with curvy women and growly shifter men who fall fast and hard, this is the holiday series for you.

Check out this instalove Christmas romance today!

Read more at https://rosebakenterprises.com/.

Also by Rose Bak

Bite-Sized Shifters
Long Distance Wolf
Wolf Doctor
Kat's Dog
Designer Wolf
Wolf Sheriff
Cocktail Wolf
Second Chance Wolf

Boozy Book Club
Beach Reads
Bubbly & Billionaires: A Midlife Instalove Romantic Comedy
Martinis & Mysteries
Bourbon & Bikers
Midlife Madness

Diamond Bay
Brand New Penny
Fresh as a Daisy
Right as Rain

Good With Numbers
Love Unmasked
The Thanksgiving Scrooge
Maid for Christmas
Countdown to Love
Valentine's Lottery
Christmas Angel

Holidays With the Shifters
Santa's Claws
Bear Humbug
Jingle Bear
Silver Paws
Joy to the Wolf
Lion's Heart

Loving the Holidays
Dating Santa
New Year's Steve
Independence Dave
Faking It with the Detective
Comfort & Joy
Dropping the Ball

Magical Midlife Romance
Love Potion

Psychic Flashes

Midlife Crisis Contemporary Romance
Summer Wedding
Roasting with Rob

Oliver Boys Band
Until You Came Along
Rock Star Teacher
Rock Star Writer
Rock Star Neighbor
Rock Star Lawyer

Reunited
Together Again
Finding My Baby

Self-Help for the Real World
It's All About Relationships

Standalone
What to Do If You Find a Cougar in Your Living Room
Beach Wedding
Good with Numbers
Christmas Love Stories: A Holiday Romance Anthology

Diamond Bay
Christmas with the Shifters

Watch for more at https://rosebakenterprises.com/.